DEATH OF A LANDLORD

NATHANIEL A. ESSEX

Published by Sufficiently Advanced Publishing LLC.

First published in 2025

ISBN 979-8-9926548-0-6

Printed in the United States of America.

For my mom, who taught me cause and effect,
which enabled me to see the future

ACKNOWLEDGMENTS

As this book is my ugly pancake, I give a special thanks to Erin McNally, Jacob R. Edlund, James Caulk, Kelly Trsek, Paul Schneider, and Scott Oltmann for taking the first bites.

For everyone else, thanks for reading...I hope it tastes better than it looks.

CHAPTER 1

Zibi buzzed her lips as she sensed the elders' fear; she always did when Eshu whispered schemes into her ear. Though she was not an elder, her father was Oba Ajaka, king of the Zadzisai Nation, and Estate Lord of thirteen planets. As Ajaka's heir and apprentice, Zibi could attend, but she could not speak.

"The barbarians have jumped thirty warships to Agu space," said Oba Tabari, king of the Igwe Nation. "The Doje disrespect the Isowo Federation. Do they make war to expand trade? No. They make war to stop trade. They make war in the name of monopoly! I say we meet him on the battlefield. I say, if Agu is too weak to stand alone, then we must bring her into the fold."

Though his sigil was the elephant, he seemed to have forgotten that once he was the mightiest Estate

Lord. When Zibi was Queen, she would attempt a monopoly as well.

As the Igwe king ranted, she reveled in her first visit to the Chamber of Elders. Circular in its design, its walls were adorned with moving murals. Each showed a different scene of where we all began and what we had become — humanity's journey through time. Men threw spears at herd animals. Ships looked down on planets. A drone army went into phalanx formation like a minefield across the galaxy.

The walls were alive with lush and tropical plants that grew towards a domed crystal ceiling. Partly cloudy windows let the sunlight in warming the chamber with its golden glow. Patterns etched into the crystal cast their shifting shadows. They danced around the table like ghosts of ancient men, who like the elders now made peace with fate.

"Heresy," said Oba Kazim of the Jelani Nation, and the other three elders nodded their agreement. "The Doje blaspheme Oduduwa, praise his name. Jakuta shames himself. He is not like his father. He is not fit to be king. Who cares for the Agu? Agu are peasants. We take the war to the Doje system and kick Jakuta on his ass!"

In unison, the elders turned to Ajaka. The Zadzisai king sat with his arms crossed, tapping a finger on the dip in his upper lip. Following a long silence, he spoke.

"Jakuta is as we once were. Oba Tabari, is it not true that they once called me tyrant? Monopolist? Oba Kazim, did I not blaspheme both Oduduwa and Obatala alike? Jakuta is what I made of him when I killed his father."

"Ajaka," said Oba Isaac of the Furaha Nation. "You did not kill that boy's parents. The landscape shifted and they could not adapt. You did not kill his family, but he certainly killed your queen."

Ajaka looked to the brilliant ceiling as if for guidance. "It was not my hand that slew them, but it was my hand that signed the document which sealed their fate and mine. The boy lashed out in anger, and look at the suffering it caused. I will not do the same. I will speak with the Agu Nation, and they will ask for aid or not."

CHAPTER 2

When the meeting adjourned, Ajaka and Zibi walked down the open corridor. Though the walkway seemed open to the elements, an artificial atmosphere generator tempered the heat. "What did you learn, Zibi?"

"That Tabari is a hypocrite, Kazim is a religious fanatic, and Isaac is a dog begging for the affection of his master."

Ajaka took a slow breath. "Be serious, Tiwa."

While Tiwa was her given name, her mother had taken to calling her Zibi because she was always buzzing her lips. A habit she had picked up from inoculating to hornet poison, as was the Zadzisai custom.

"Jakuta brings war to the Agu Nation because they are weakened from supply shortages. Which is why you should let me send a fleet to defend Agu."

"Why are there shortages?"

"Because they must refuel in Nwadike space and the Nwadike are like bridge trolls who demand outrageously high taxes for their fuel stations."

"Why do they tax so much?"

"Because they are rent-seeking brigands."

"What is the strategic value to being a rent-seeking brigand?"

"Power. To get something for nothing."

"Why do they want this power?"

"So, they can be favored by the Doje."

"Why do they want the favor of the Doje?"

"So, they don't get conquered next."

"So, what did you learn, Zibi?"

"The Doje use economics as a weapon, like archers softening the battlefield. Then they send in soldiers to drain the Agu's resources until they can no longer sustain the fight. Which is why I would send a fleet to assist the Agu. Call it a display of force. The Doje would not dare make war with us."

Ajaka stopped and Zibi followed his lead. He stared out at the gardens of the palace, his eyes tracing over the greenery and flowing water.

"To believe we are infallible because we are the biggest is folly. That is a gentle lie we tell ourselves. A hard truth is better than a gentle lie. You will make a fine Queen someday. But today, I want you to stay out of this."

"But—"

"Promise me."

"But—"

Ajaka's face was like a marble statue.

She nodded. Then he nodded and kissed her forehead, leaving her alone in the garden. Then as soon as her father was out of sight, she called her spymaster.

"Sima, I want you to hire a mercenary fleet."

CHAPTER 3

People packed the bazaar landscape, with local, foreign, and domestic color. Painted lords, steel-toothed thieves, and beggars wearing nothing but their bones.

From prophet gymnosophists to panhandling swine, all the peoples wore their sigils proudly. Some on headscarves, some on sleeves, they fastened buckles and glistened rings. Brilliant, dull, trendy, classic, their tribe's totem was power.

Whenever she came to visit Sima, Zibi hid her hornet hairpin with a hood. Industrious and deadly, a fly upon the wall, Zibi had ears on every world and Sima was their mouthpiece. She ate some sweets, breathed in the spice, and swayed to drum and string. And just as she got comfortable, she felt a hornet sting.

"Yow!" Zibi screamed and Sima doubled over with laughter.

"You are so soft," Sima said, throwing an arm around Zibi's neck. "If you were an ancient, you would surely be eaten by a lion."

Unamused, Zibi walked away. She tried to look commonplace and keep her face concealed. Despite her mild annoyance, Sima's familiarity reduced the onlookers' suspicion. Royalty amongst the commonwealth was all too common, but these were desperate times.

Sima hurried after her friend, employer, cousin, after paying a vendor for some fruit. When no apology was forthcoming, Zibi reiterated her need.

"I did not call you here to play, Sima. I want to hire a—"

"A mercenary fleet. Yes, I heard you. But that, sister, is a terrible idea."

Zibi frowned. "The Doje are already in Agu space, they could strike at any time. Every independent planet the Doje take, they become even more distrustful. The greater their distrust, the higher their prices."

Sima shook her head, spitting chunks of apple as she spoke. "You know you should just marry Jakuta."

CHAPTER 4

Zibi jumped as if she had been stung again. "What?"
"It's the quickest way to end hostilities," said
Sima, extending the fruit like an olive branch. "Hear
me out. By joining with the Jakuta, you bind the two
largest alliances in the Isowo Federation."

"But he—"

"I know," Sima said softly. "I know what he did
to your mother. I also know that nothing can change
the past. If you look to the future, you will see only
opportunity."

Zibi stopped at a jewelry stall and held a golden
blown glass necklace to the sky. "I see the opportunity
to both earn goodwill with the independents and to
strike at the man who murdered my mother in cold
blood."

The princess put the amulet against her chest.

"Then look a little closer, oh wise and beautiful Zibi. Who is this man Jakuta? What do you know of him beyond his crimes?"

"He is a warlord. He is a tyrant. He seeks only power for himself."

Zibi purchased the necklace and tipped the vendor a handsome premium.

"Warlord, tyrant, power. What are these words? What he is, what he seeks, not who he is, why he seeks it. He is a man of determination. He is cunning in strategy. He commands respect when he speaks...and he is also quite handsome."

The princess curled her lip at the thought of being in the room with the tyrant king, let alone a betrothal to him.

"Think Zibi," said Sima. "The alliance would allow your father to mold him. It would allow you to tame him. Remember Scheherazade?"

The story was ancient among the ancients. The Yamandulo, the old ones who were one tribe of many peoples, had a story of a tyrant king. He married his advisor's daughter and every night she told him stories. They softened his heart and sharpened his mind and made of him a great king.

Zibi touched the jewel on her throat and spoke through clenching teeth. "We are not the Yamandulo, and I am not Scheherazade. I am Tiwa, heir to the Zadzisai throne."

Sima bowed her head. "Yes, milady."

"I will hear no more discussion of arranged marriages," said Zibi, her authority towering over her subject. "You will hire me a fleet to defend the Agu, and you will send me your choice of admiral before the setting sun."

Sima never failed.

CHAPTER 5

After hiring the most fearsome mercenary in the Zadzisai nation, Zibi celebrated with a glass of honeyed wine. Her ship traversed the twilight sky, the bazaar a twinkling afterthought. She unfastened her seatbelt as the ship entered orbit and paced around the cabin, her mind buzzing with decisions and deals.

The small sips of wine had done nothing to settle her, so she drank until she could sit. She stared out the window at the planet below, stretched out like electric blue glass. The curve of the horizon shone in a soft arc, the sun burning brilliant on the day side. She touched the glass necklace that glittered in gold. She would purchase new worlds, but home never grew old.

Exiting orbit, beginning descent, the palace was a lighthouse from space. The estate grounds grew nearer, its gardens grew greener, and so did guard towers and guns. Despite the fortress and impressive threat display, the dangers inside were more deadly. Suddenly, a buzzing sound startled Zibi into alertness. It was a message from a local informant.

"What is it?" Zibi asked the informant. "Could this not wait until I land?"

"I am sorry, milady. I thought you might want to go straight to the Umantyi Courthouse."

The Umantyi were a quasi-religious order that blessed contracts and mediated international disputes. As the Isowo Federation was a Free Market Democracy, each kingdom was subject to their own laws. Thus, the Umantyi were an impartial third party to any and all legally binding contracts.

"Was there a—" Zibi hiccupped and covered her mouth.

"You told me to inform you of any news regarding your father's movements and—"

Then as the ship descended toward the landing platform, she understood why the guards were on full display.

"Is that a Doje corvette?"

"Ma'am?"

"Why is there a Doje warship on my landing pad?"

"That is what I was trying to tell you, Ajaka is about to meet with Jakuta."

CHAPTER 6

Zibi opened her mouth to speak, but felt acid burning her throat. The implications were dire. While no one would dare bring violence inside an Umantyi courthouse, the steps outside were a commonplace for murder and betrayal.

Though the informant continued to speak, venom welled in Zibi's cheeks and fury burned in her gut. She snarled and gritted her teeth at the thought of Jakuta on her homeworld. She wanted to scratch his eyes out, to peel the skin from his hands. She wanted to brand him with iron and stone him one pebble at a time. She wanted to... She wanted to... She wanted to be with her father. She needed to protect him.

Her fingers tightened around her passport.

"Why didn't he tell me?" Zibi whispered to herself. Why didn't he trust her?

The ship landed and Zibi ran. The courthouse was not far, and her mind raced. Why in space would Jakuta arrange this meeting?

She knew where Ajaka would be, preparing in his private chamber. She only had a few minutes before he would leave for court. She hoped that was enough time to change his mind.

As she approached his office, the guards lowered their spears.

"What is the meaning of this?" She said aghast at their audacity.

"Orders of the king, milady. No one is to disturb the Oba, not even you, princess."

"Father!" Zibi shouted. "Let me in! I must speak with you!"

But there was no response. So, she waited for an eternity. Three minutes later the chamber door opened.

"Father," she said coolly, masking her anxiety. Ajaka looked up, a flicker of surprise unhidden from his eyes.

"Zibi, you should not be here," he said.

"I know, but I wanted to wish you well," she lied.

Stepping closer, she hugged him for a long moment. He handed his tablet to an aide and embraced her.

"Have you been drinking?"

"Maybe. Just a little. Did you sleep at all last night?" she said, changing the subject.

"Maybe. Just a little."

She could feel the smile in his voice.

"Why didn't you tell me about Jakuta?" She whispered.

"Why didn't you tell me about the fleet?" he whispered back.

"I was afraid for you," she said.

"And I was afraid for you."

Tears welled in Zibi's eyes.

"Peace, my dear, Tiwa. I will explain everything when the business is done. Can you trust that an old lion still has a trick or two?"

Ajaka wiped Zibi's face, and she straightened the collar of his robe.

"Be careful, father. You know we cannot trust him."

Ajaka smiled. "Trust goes both ways, my love. It must be earned by both parties. I will earn his trust and give him the opportunity to earn mine."

She nodded.

"Stay safe and stay hidden. You are a gift," he said and Zibi nodded again.

Oba Ajaka strode down the corridor with his entourage, his presence radiant as a sun. Then just as her father was out of sight, Zibi tested the sound quality of the bug she had planted on his collar.

CHAPTER 7

The Umantyi Courthouse dripped with grandeur, its design both menacing and graceful. The facade was a voidish obsidian called Omotayo Stone. This Yamandulo material reflected the surrounding landscape but seemed to devour the sunlight. All Umantyi structures were made of this rare and sacred substance. The Umantyi courts were made from it and so was the army of drones that stood sentinel across the galaxy. No one would harm an Umantyi because no one would survive the reckoning.

The courtroom itself was arranged in concentric circles. The judge sat at the center on an elevated throne of carved ebony with golden leaf and filigree. Like the chamber of elders, there was a domed ceiling. But instead of crystal, a moving mural depicted the heavens. Stars and constellations yielded to celestial beings.

Gods of sun and moon. Gods of eternity and fate. The gods Oduduwa and Obatala, they watched the proceedings below. And hidden among the kings of gods, Zibi watched from her hornet cam.

At the center of this grand chamber stood Jakuta. He was tall and imposing, his presence as commanding as a mountain range, and to Zibi's shame, he was handsome. But his eyes were cold and hostile, cunning, alert, and deadly.

"Three planets," Jakuta stated, his voice echoing through the chamber. "Give them to me, and the Doje will withdraw from Agu."

The offer was outrageous of course. Those planets were vital to the Zadzisai nation, both strategically and culturally. Losing them would hamper trade and embolden the Doje further. Yet Ajaka, seated opposite Jakuta nodded as if this was expected.

After deliberating for a long moment, Ajaka said with a steady voice, "What if I were to offer you a betrothal to my daughter, Tiwa?"

"What?" Zibi shouted.

She had found a quiet alcove in the grand hallway of the courthouse to listen in on her father's negotiation. More than a few passersby startled at her exclamation.

"This union would bind our tribes, in a more meaningful way. This would make both of us far stronger than any territorial concession I could provide to you. Greater even than you could gain for yourself, I think."

CHAPTER 8

"No, no, no!" All hell and fury, Zibi watched like a tampered jury.

Jakuta's eyes narrowed. To marry the Zadzisai princess would give him a near monopoly upon Ajaka's death. It seemed like a trap, even to Zibi, but Jakuta's pride was legendary.

But if Jakuta's pride was legend, Zibi's was a force of nature. To be tied forever to her sworn enemy, was too bitter a pill to swallow. Before she knew it, she was on her feet, heels clicking down the hall toward the courtroom.

"This is not going to happen, father," Zibi said to the passport screen. "Sima will not decide who I marry, and neither will you!"

As Jakuta mulled over the offer, a faint commotion could be heard from outside the chamber. It grew louder as she approached, realizing then she was shouting. With the echoing feedback in her earpiece, Zibi shut off the bug.

The guards at the entrance exchanged uneasy glances. Their hands shaky on their spears. "Princess, the court is in session, you — "

Zibi kicked open the grand doors of the courtroom even as the guards lifted her off her feet.

"Unhand me!" She screamed. "Father, I will not stand for it!"

She couldn't as she was literally floating in the guards' grip.

"You cannot barter away our people's future!"

Ajaka turned to her, his head cocked with curious amusement. "Let her be. Tiwa, the deal is done."

Then she saw; the judge's seal glowed over the negotiating table. The contract had been blessed.

"Zibi, this is our chance for peace." The plea in his voice was clear as water, but Zibi felt ice in her veins.

The guards unhanded her, and she rushed toward Ajaka. But before she could reach him, Jakuta rose from his seat, his face a mask of fury. Then without warning, his hand shot out, gripping the hilt of a dagger. The motion was swift, but it seemed slow to Zibi. His blade plunged into Ajaka's back.

Her father turned to look at his killer, satisfaction on the brigand's face. Ajaka raised a hand, blood falling from the corners of his mouth. He touched Jakuta's face with an affection Zibi could not understand.

"Be good, my son..." he coughed blood and fell to his knees. "...be good, for you are loved."

Then Jakuta stabbed Ajaka in his heart.

CHAPTER 9

"We have to go," Sima hissed, grabbing Zibi's arm. Zibi resisted but when Jakuta's gaze fell upon her, she fled.

Tears streaming down her face, Zibi allowed herself to be led. Sima propelled them through the corridors of the courthouse, away from the bloodshed and into the night. They boarded an unmarked ship and were out of the system within the hour.

An old Yamandulo proverb says, "we do not rise to the level of our expectation but fall to our level of training." Zibi had known Ajaka's assassination was a possibility, and she had prepared. Thus, despite her distress, she charted a course to the one man she could trust.

Bankole's modest home sat on the outskirts of the capital systems, on the planet farthest from the sun, in the heart of a secluded forest. The retired Umantyi judge retained his diplomatic immunity but had lost his taste for politics. With her father gone, Zibi hoped he would share some wisdom from his half century of mergers, acquisitions, and hostile takeovers.

The gate was open, so she entered the compound. The door was open, so she entered the house. Inside, she found Bankole seated at a low table, chatting with a servant who prepared a simple meal. He wore a robe with animal furs, as it was cold despite the burning fireplace.

"Ah, Tiwa, my child. I have been expecting you."

Zibi's eyes filled with tears, and she rushed to embrace her friend. "He's gone uncle. He's gone."

The old man cooed and rubbed her back. "I know, child, I know. You are safe now."

Releasing the old man, Zibi shook her head. "I fear I will never be safe again. Jakuta has--that bastard! I'm going to — "

"Peace, child. Peace."

"Uncle, I need your help. We have no time to waste."

Bankole looked into Zibi's eyes, his expression gentle, but unreadable. "Zibi," he said, with a generous smile, "You are always in such a hurry. I was just about to have lunch. Be a darling and help Abi prepare the meal. Then we will talk."

Zibi's frustration boiled over. "This is more important than brunch!" She insisted, "My father has just died!" Her eyes flicked over to Abi, who remained focused on his task. "Please, Bankole. I need your help now." She lowered her voice to a whisper. "And I do not know this man."

Bankole nodded. "I understand. But this is the deal. If you want my advice, then help Abi prepare the meal and then help clean up afterward." Then quoting Yamandulo scripture, he said, "Manners maketh man."

CHAPTER 10

Bankole was not just an ally, but Ajaka's closest friend. How could he be so dismissive? After all that had happened, he expected her to add insult to injury by scrubbing pots and pans with the help? Zibi's fists clenched, but the set of Bankole's jaw told her he wasn't going to budge. The room fell silent, but for the soft clinking of utensils coming from the kitchen.

Zibi stood. "I will help with the meal." She declared as if issuing a formal proclamation.

"A dignified choice," said the elder.

Beneath her anger, Zibi felt a growing realization that Bankole was testing her. Ajaka had once said "there is no such thing as a difficult test if you know all the answers." But she didn't know all the answers. Therefore, she needed to study.

Zibi joined Abi in the kitchen. "What are we making?"

"Maafe. It is mostly done. Would you stir that, so it does not stick?" Abi pointed to a pot on the stovetop.

Zibi did as asked.

"Thank you." Abi stopped his task and turned to face her. "I am sorry to hear about your father. He was a great man."

She was not eager to discuss family matters or politics with the peasantry, but she could at least be polite. "Thank you."

Abi returned to chopping bell peppers and sweet potatoes.

"I saw him three times. The first was when I was a boy. He had just acquired the whole of the Bantu Nation via hostile takeover. I was attending court with my father. He was so powerful, with jewels and servants everywhere. I said 'baba, who is that man?' And my father said, 'that man is ajogun. You must learn from him.'"

Another religious fanatic. Followers of Obatala and Oduduwa were always talking about egungun and ajogun, angels and demons. Zibi had no time for superstitious nonsense.

Abi dumped the diced vegetables into the stew and then mixed the rice.

"Then as a young man, after my father had passed, I met him. I was with my mother at the market following the war that decimated the Furaha nation. Like us, he was there on a mission of charity. I saw him personally handing out food to Furaha refugees. My mother said, 'that man is egungun. You must learn from him.'"

That was the man Zibi knew. A man of peace and charity. It chafed her to think of her father as a tyrant. She had studied his acquisitions and though he had made hostile takeovers, he never started a war. They were always in retaliation to his effective negotiations.

The two began setting the table.

"When was the third time you met my father?"

Abi smiled. "Just a few days ago. We mostly talked about you."

None of her spies had mentioned this.

"You actually spoke to him?"

"Of course, he did." Bankole interjected. "Now, since you have honored your word and helped prepare this marvelous feast, I will honor my end of the bargain as well. Allow me to introduce Oba Abiodun, king of the Onyilogwu Nation, Estate Lord of Alkebulan. And my advice is that you should marry him."

CHAPTER 11

Royals were owed respect, but Zibi was queen of the Zadzisai and Abi was a backwater king. She curtsied but did not kneel. She would bend the knee to no one.

"Proud girl," said Bankole, "you know so much, yet see so little."

Zibi couldn't suppress the scowl.

"My face is not known, uncle." Then Abi knelt and prostrated himself, kissing Zibi's feet. He sat up to a kneeling position and smiled earnestly. "I am a minor lord. I have no ambitions beyond the safety of my people. Your father invited me to the capital system several weeks ago to tell me of his plans. I was disguised as a gardener."

That's what those long walks were about. His long gaze at the garden after the elder's meeting...Was he looking at Abi?

"The old lion had many tricks," Bankole chuckled. "I think I will miss him, but then I see him in you."

Abi rose and began serving the food.

Zibi's annoyance grew at their nonchalance. "Does anyone care to share this elaborate plan with me? I am betrothed to Jakuta. The man who has murdered both of my parents. And now he hunts me. Surely, he will kill me next or torture me by forcing me to have his child while he ruins my father's legacy."

"That was not the deal," said Bankole, passing her a tablet. "The Umantyi alumni network is strong. I have the contract here."

She scanned the document.

"You see? You are betrothed to Jakuta, but he gains no claim to the Zadzisai until you accept his proposal."

Zibi shook her head. "No. Until I accept his proposal or that of another." She read the clause.

"In the event the LADY declines to marry the GENTLEMAN and enters into a binding marriage contract with another individual, all rights to the aforementioned assets shall be forfeit to the GENTLEMAN. Thenceforth, the LADY shall not be entitled to any claim over the assets."

"That was the deal," said Bankole.

"Why in heaven would he make such a deal?"

"For your happiness," said Abi.

"What do you know?" Zibi spat.

"I know what it is to be responsible for a nation and to love individuals." Abi continued. "Sometimes the duty to the many must come before the love of the one. But if you are clever and resourceful, you can bind your love and duty together."

"Abi is right," said Bankole, "Ajaka was no fool. Jakuta is powerful, but if he were to attack the Zadzisai, he would lose. Even without him, the elders will not stand for Doje butchery. He believed at best that you and Jakuta could reshape the galaxy together. His might and your wisdom would make a great alliance. But if marrying your mother's murderer was too much for you, then you could choose your own path."

"But this is no choice at all!"

"Oh child, what do you lose? Whatever you decide, you are still a queen. Whatever you decide, you will not be hunted. Whatever you decide, you are free to pursue your own happiness. Ajaka was willing to give the whole of the Zadzisai Nation to the Doje, so his only daughter could live the life she chose."

"Marry me," said Abi, "I know we have just met, but I can see the egungun in you. And I can be quite charming. Given time, you may even grow affection for me."

Ajaka had thought of nearly everything. But she was not some pawn, she was the Zadzisai queen. The proposal of an elopement was well-meaning, but it wasn't the solution she needed.

"Abi, Oba, I appreciate your offer," she began, "But I cannot accept it. Without my dowry, it is only a matter of time before the Doje seize control of the entire Isowo Federation. My people will be in danger as long as Jakuta lives."

Back in the civilized world, on the Igwe capital planet, inside the grandiose hall, Zibi met Oba Tabari who sat his ebony throne. Storm clouds gathered as thunder drummed outside. The air was thick with incense, the walls were lined with pride. Elephants and ivory, power and tradition. Zibi knelt before the elder, his eyes dark with perdition.

"Oba Tabari," Zibi began, her voice urgent yet steady, "I come seeking your wisdom. By taking Ajaka's life, Jakuta pits himself against us. The Doje threaten the stability of the Federation, and so in the name of our alliance, I ask that you help me stop him before it is too late."

Tabari's eyes remained fixed on her as a lion upon a calf. Then he leaned back in his seat. "Oba Tiwa," he replied, his voice hungry and deliberate. "You speak of 'our' alliance, but I have no recollection of making any deals with you."

CHAPTER 12

Zibi had expected resistance, but she hadn't anticipated this. How could Tabari be so stupid as to
break up the alliance with the Doje at his door?

"The alliance is with the Zadzisai Nation and as
the head of the—"

"My alliance was with Ajaka. I did not make an
alliance with the Zadzisai people. I did not make an
alliance with a little girl who cannot chart the stars. No.
I made a deal with Ajaka and Ajaka is dead."

"The alliance between you and Ajaka has stood
for nearly a decade. If you no longer recognize it, then
perhaps we can make a new deal."

A toothpick materialized in Tabari's hand from
somewhere in his robes. "You speak as if this alliance were a noble thing. But do you know how it was
forged?"

It was a rhetorical question, so Zibi waited. The king dug a morsel of some unknown cuisine from his molars and sucked the toothpick clean.

Then the king leaned forward, menace in his tone. "Ajaka was once like Jakuta—ambitious, cunning, ruthless."

Lies. Ajaka fought for the prosperity of his people.

"He made clever trades, not war. He found opportunity where others would not look."

Tabari laughed. "Of course he made no war. He had no army to speak of. It was not his brilliant trades that put him on the throne. It was his assassins."

"That's not..." Zibi hesitated. Tabari hated liars and Zibi didn't know if what he said was true.

"Ah, I see uncertainty in you. Ajaka forced me into this alliance by seizing four of my territories and murdering three of my closest friends. You come to me with your beggar's cup, but Ajaka did not ask for help. He took what he wanted and the rest of us had to take the scraps or die. That is your father's legacy. A bright and shining ship that sails a sea of blood."

Struggling to retain her composure, Zibi's voice was small as she spoke. "I am not my father."

Then suddenly, the ferocity fled from Tabari's eyes. "No, child. No, you are not." The king drew in a breath and released it. When he spoke again, his voice had softened and sounded almost regretful. "I am sorry for your loss. The man your father became..." But Tabari stopped himself from finishing. As if remembering himself, he straightened and affected his royal tone. "Your intentions may be noble, but the blood of Ajaka flows through your veins. Your hands, child, are your father's hands. And only when a child has cleaned her hands may she eat at my table."

CHAPTER 13

Frustrated by her defeat, Zibi tried and failed to contact the Furaha Nation. Tabari was the most powerful of her father's allies, but Isaac was the most loyal. Every attempt to reach him was met with silence. She needed allies and resources, and she needed them fast, so she set course for Jelani space.

Zibi had hoped to have Tabari and Isaac's support before meeting with Kazim. Oba Kazim had always seemed more interested in pretty things than politics. She might have to offer him a tropical world to even get his attention.

Kazim's palace was a gaudy thing. Surrounded by lush gardens and towering skyscrapers that twinkled with jewels like stars. As she was escorted to the grand hall, she tried to suppress her disgust. The walls were gilded gold, the floors were polished marble, the walls were marred with moving murals of buxom busts and orgies. Beneath the splendor and oversized opulence, she felt like eyes were on her. Hidden on every mural, behind every scene, a squirrel stole a nut or grape like the thief she'd come to see.

Oba Kazim greeted Zibi with a smile that got close, but didn't quite reach his eyes. He beckoned for her to sit at a long table where a feast had been prepared. Despite the abundance, Kazim's palace felt like a casino, like every bite would cost her.

"Welcome, welcome," the king began, "I am sorry to hear about your father. Ajaka was a great man. I fashioned my kingdom from his example."

This gaudy monstrosity was nothing like her father's shining city on a hill. But she appreciated the compliment.

"How was your trip?" He asked.

"It was pleasant enough, thank you."

"And the service? How did you find the staff?"

"They were fine."

"Just fine? On a scale of one to ten..."

"Uh," Zibi tried to be honest, but didn't want to give a poor review. "Perhaps an 8."

"Ah, splendid," Kazim said. Then he snapped his fingers, and a young man rushed over to his high-backed chair like a ballboy in a tennis match. The king whispered something and the boy's face blanched. After shewing the servant away, Kazim returned his attention to Zibi. "So, how can I be of service?"

"Jakuta. First he martials his forces against the Agu, and now, I fear he has gone to war with Furaha."

After her failure with Tabari, Zibi decided on a more direct approach. "If we do not join forces, now, we will both be crushed."

Kazim tapped his fingers on the arm of his chair. The longer he tapped, the more Zibi was convinced it was the rhythm to a pop song. "You ask so much, Oba Tiwa," he said in a smooth seductive tone. "But I am a reasonable man. I will help you."

"Really?" She blurted out incredulously.

"Yes. I think Jakuta is godless heathen, and he needs to be stopped before he destabilizes the entire Federation."

"On this we can agree. Clearly, his strategy is to separate us, pick us off one at a time."

"My thoughts exactly. If you can open the fist, you can bite off the fingers." He continued tapping that annoying rhythm and the tune sprung to Zibi's mind.

"Precisely. In addition to the Zadzisai fleet, I have hired a mercenary company to add to our forces. They can distract the Nwadike, you can take on the Mmeremikwu and I will take on the Doje's main host."

"A brilliant plan. You are an excellent strategist, just like your father. Oduduwa shines in you."

Zibi beamed.

"We will commence with all haste. But first, you must cede the Olola system to me. Consider this interest on the five planets your father took from my portfolio years ago. Second, you will marry my youngest son. This will solidify our alliance and bind us forever in the eyes of the gods."

CHAPTER 14

Disgust welled up in Zibi's gut and she tried to force it down. The man's greed hung in the air like smog. His ambition was limitless, his hospitality a veneer. He cared nothing for the Zadzisai or for her family. All this man wanted was his cut.

How could her father have allied with such a man? He pretended to be pious, but it was all just a coercive scheme. She knew of his sons by reputation only. They were a pack of hyenas. Tales of their debaucherous sex clone shop had been fodder for tabloids since the eldest boy came of age. The idea of marrying one of them made her stomach turn.

Zibi rose from her seat, her voice resolved. "Oba Kazim, I thank you for your hospitality, but unfortunately I cannot agree to your terms. The Olola system houses my home and capital world. In it resides the strength of my people. I cannot, I will not sacrifice them — or myself — on such an altar. What I can offer are discounted rates at all Zadzisai ports, and tax-free accommodations to all Jelani citizens for the next five years."

Kazim's smile only widened. "I'm afraid you misunderstand your position, Oba Tiwa."

He waved a hand, and two armor-plated Mamluks surrounded Zibi. Then a squad of over a dozen soldiers relieved her royal guard of their weaponry.

"You will stay here and enjoy my hospitality until you have reconsidered your decision. We will speak again in the morning."

Zibi was escorted from the great hall to the sound of boots on marble and Kazim whistling that damnable pop song.

CHAPTER 15

Kazim's hospitality was an extravagant rug thrown over the filth coating the floor. Since Kazim had provided neither bed nor chair, Zibi stood amidst that filth in the center of her cell.

The stone walls were covered in something slick and putrid. Steam pipes lined the halls outside, the dungeon must have been beneath the sewage system. That would explain the smell. Water dripped and she hugged her knees, trying and failing to hide from despair.

She would not submit. She would not marry. Not this tyrant nor that. At least Kazim pretended to be kind, Jakuta would just stab her in the chest. Fury had taken root and grown like firegrass in her mind, she lifted her gaze as the iron door opened and she prepared to unleash her fury.

Sima stepped into the cell, her white teeth brightening the dark. "I was right about you. If you had lived with the ancients, you would certainly be eaten by a lion."

Sima played savior for the second time this week, and Zibi was spirited away. They winded their way through Kazim's fortress bowels, hidden from his guards by his servants. The women moved in silence, like shadows hugging walls, confounding surveillance systems with hornet tech.

Once outside the fortress, they entered a patch of thick trees where Sima had hidden her shuttle. It wasn't until they were offworld, out of the system, and back in Zadzisai space that Zibi could finally breathe.

"Thank you, Sima," she said. "I thought I would have to burn the palace to the ground."

She hugged her cousin then, but Sima pushed her away with a bitter scowl.

"Girl, you stink. Get cleaned up and then we can embrace for real." Then her smile returned and Zibi laughed for the first time in ages. Zibi turned to leave, but Sima stopped her.

"There is one thing, I must say before too much time has passed." The spymaster's voice became serious. "It's the Furaha Nation... they're gone. Completely absorbed by the Doje." Sima's gaze fell to the floor. "Oba Isaac is dead."

CHAPTER 16

Zibi had called Isaac a dog, but he was truly loyal and without him, she begged for scraps.

She sank to the floor and hugged her knees. She had never left that prison cell. The walls were no longer coated with slime, the floor no longer cold. Where could she run when the whole of the galaxy was her cage?

Her body trembled as she tried to stifle her sobs. She rocked herself and buzzed her lips to drown out her father's last words. They weren't even to her. Then she allowed herself the tears.

Zibi felt a hand on her back, and she fell into it. "I know sister, I know." Sima held her queen as she cried.

"I've lost it—" Zibi struggled to breathe, "Everything, I've—" She couldn't get a breath. She looked at Sima, her eyes wide. "My father...everything he built...

over a lifetime." She clutched her chest. "I have lost it in days... I am a queen with no kingdom, no power, and no way to protect my people."

Kneeling beside her, arms wrapped around her, Sima made a rare showing of herself. "I know it feels hopeless," she said, "but you are still here. You are still fighting. And that means we still have a chance. We just need the right opportunity."

Zibi wiped her tears, struggling to regain her composure. Sima was right. But what could she do? The Furaha were gone. The other tribes were either preparing for war or making deals with the Doje.

She had only one path left, the gift Ajaka had given her. Zibi's voice grew strong, and she said, "Set a course for Bankole's house."

When they arrived, Bankole checked his wristwatch. "All things considered, I would say you learned rather quickly."

Abi stood nearby, his expression less excitement and more...relief?

Zibi approached him. She looked down at the floor and knelt. Resigned and resolved, she sealed her fate. "Oba Abiodun Onyilogwu, Oba Tiwa Zadzisai accepts your proposal. I will marry you."

Then Abi did a curious thing. He squatted down and sat on the floor. He took one of Zibi's hands in his and with the other, he cupped her face. "I will do everything in my power to protect you and our people."

CHAPTER 17

In the middle of nowhere, in a chill dark forest, the wedding was nothing like Zibi had imagined. In her youth, she had pictured an outdoor event, but on the palace grounds. This planet belonged to the independent nation of Keita and had become a haven for vagabonds and exiles. This continent was nearly all uninhabited forest replete with soggy marshes and such dense canopy it blotted out the sun. But if spies were watching from space, they would be harder to pick up with direct or thermal scanning.

She imagined being surrounded by family as Oba Ajaka gave her away to some suave and powerful king. Abi was tall and thick with rough hands like he had bred cattle his whole life. For all she knew, he had.

The priest would speak from scripture, and they would exchange vows. They'd kiss and then retreat to a tropical honeymoon on Baja or Haitia or Bogo. But her father was dead. Sima and Bankole were the only ones to witness the official document signing.

The Umantyi judge wore water resistant denim instead of his traditional robes. Bankole trusted him, so Zibi had no choice but to trust him too. Regardless, they had their ship on standby in case they needed to run.

"Once the marriage contract is signed and uploaded, Jakuta will be alerted. The Doje will likely send forces to collect or dispose of you." Said the elder. Had to hand it to the Umantyi, they were always to the point. "Are you ready?"

Zibi's gaze flickered to Abi, and he smiled, his calm demeanor offering little comfort. "Yes." She sighed and then she signed.

Once the judge had blessed the contract and the documents were uploaded to the cloud, the atmosphere shifted. Zibi's blood ran cold. Before she could fully process the feeling, the overcast sky began to darken.

Zibi turned to Sima. "Run!"

She and Sima all sprinted toward the ship. Abi went back to support the two elders, one on each arm. A low rumble reverberated through the ground, causing Zibi's feet to sink into the bog. As they entered the clearing, she saw the Doje warships, like black winged demons upon the horizon.

"Launch!" Zibi screamed as soon as the elders were inside. With all haste the shuttle took off. Everything went in slow motion. They strapped in. They exited the atmosphere. They arrived in the hangar bay of the cloaked imperial cruiser. Zibi looked out the window and saw fiery trails, they streaked toward the planet's surface. Like hateful angry meteor showers, they extinguished the planet from orbit.

CHAPTER 18

The Yamandulo had a saying that war was hell. Ajaka had once said this was not true. In fact, war is worse than hell. Because in hell it is only the guilty who suffer.

Zibi watched the planet burn as she fled. The ship entered the portal and suddenly they were out of Keita space. No more Doje warships. No more burning planet. No more Zadzisai. Just the familiar Yamandulo phalanx, draped across the cosmos.

Jakuta would never stop hunting her, so long as she was alive. Perhaps it was for the best if he believed she had died on that planet. As the ship approached Alkebulan, Zibi wept for who she had been.

"Zibi?" said a calm voice.

"Tiwa," she replied, her gaze never leaving the window.

"Tiwa?" Abi said again, "how can I support you?"

Tiwa turned to face her husband. "Help me destroy my enemies. Burn them from the skies. Rain fire upon their very souls, to pay for all their crimes."

CHAPTER 19

As their ship descended onto Alkebulan, Tiwa gazed out at a world lost to time. Rolling hills of violet and gold, wheat and wildflower, brilliant and bold, baobab trees looked over the fold, they reached for the sky like guardians of old. The rivers, they sparkled and wound through the valleys, they fed into lakes like crystalline alleys. And then she saw people and they worked the land. They picked and they tilled with dirt on their hands. Nothing was touched by chaos or war. Everything alive, nothing ignored.

Tiwa felt a seed of hope sprout in her chest, but she smothered it. She was not a girl, but a queen. And hope was not a strategy.

Stepping out onto the soil, they were greeted by a parade of villagers who bowed and offered them welcome. Tiwa felt immediately ashamed that she had never studied the Onyilogwu in earnest. She knew they lived simply, in harmony with the land, preferring tradition to technology. But she felt out of place here, in her regal attire, which seemed gaudy as Oba Kazim's counterfeit palace.

Abi held her hand and guided her through the crowd. The people hugged him and kissed his cheeks. They congratulated him on his marriage and lauded the beauty of his queen. Men jostled him by the shoulder and playfully punched his chest. They welcomed him home like a conquering hero. And Tiwa felt pride in her breast.

Those satisfied feelings fled quickly as Tiwa was humbled by pain. Everyone rose before dawn, working fields from morning til night. They toiled under the heat of the sun, working with little respite. The labor was tireless, relentless—digging trenches, hauling water, grinding grain. Tiwa had spent her whole life in board rooms. She was unaccustomed to pain.

Her once soft hands, like unblemished silk, became bruised and calloused and raw. Every muscle and joint ached, her back screamed and cried, and her mind unraveled like twine. Oh, how she longed for a comfortable couch, a movie, some candy, and wine.

But it was not the days that humbled the hornet, twas the night that gnawed at her soul. She fell asleep fast, from her body's fatigue, and that's when the terrors began. Jakuta killed her mother and father again and again on repeat. An endless loop of love lost, dread, despair, death, and defeat.

She had never left Bankole's planet. She watched the missiles streak toward her. Animals ran, but they couldn't run fast enough, so they burned. She felt the heat melting her flesh as Jakuta laughed aloud.

He hunted her through grass and plains, with loin cloth, spear and rage. She ran, she cowered, cursed and cried, the whole planet her cage. Hunted like a beast, like on the elder's chamber wall. He threw his spear, it pierced her back, she braced herself to fall. She landed on her knees and tried to breathe. She did her best. But the spear tip cleaved her lung and sprouted from her chest. Just like the knife that took the life and broke Ajaka's heart. Father, can't you see he was a snake right from the start. Jakuta bore anaconda sigils, mad, wild and depraved, then dragged her screaming, by her hair, back to his midnight cave.

CHAPTER 20

One night, Tiwa awoke in a pool of sweat, and trying not to wake Abi she stumbled to the door.

"Tiwa?" came the voice from behind her. "Your dreams are a symptom. They will stop if—"

Superstitious backwater magic. Breath ragged, she shook her head as she bolted. She ran down the curving steps, across the foyer floor. Barefoot, she fled the manor house, crashed into the double doors. She ran into the moonless night—it felt so like a dream. Her feet unfettered as she flew, she had no time to feel. She ran from dreams in life anew, uncertain what was real.

She would leave this place behind. It had nothing for her. Only her life. What good was it while the Federation burned? She had taken to snapping at people during the day. They didn't seem to care. They didn't care about the war. They didn't care that their queen was suffering. They didn't care about her father.

She heard them whisper behind her back. She knew what they told their children.

Ajogun.

Wicked. Demon. Spirit of the dark. She must have seemed as much as she tore through the black of night.

These pious peasants. Couldn't they see? She was suffering. She wasn't a demon.

Just then she spotted a light from inside the hangar.

The shuttle's lights were on. Could it be a thief? She searched herself, dumbly. Her nightgown had no pockets.

What did it matter? Maybe the thief would ransom her to Jakuta, and she could get close enough to slit his throat. Tiwa pressed forward.

To her surprise, she found Sima sitting in the cockpit and sharpening a blade. Her hair was nappy and frazzled. Her head nodded back and forth as she mumbled out an incoherent banter with herself.

"Sima?"

Sima startled and pointed her blade.

Tiwa raised her hands. "Couldn't sleep?"

The spymaster nodded and lowered the knife. "Obatala curses this place. It's the Ase. The Ase is dark in this place. Dark... Ajogun in the dark."

She had never seen Sima like this. Something was very wrong.

"What are you talking about? What is the Ase?"

"Ase is power. Ase is the magic of the universe, the life of the gods that flows through us, the true magic, the god magic, the power. Ase is the power. Ase is the power. The power of the gods. The gods curse this place. Curse this place, curse this place, curse this place..."

Tiwa approached cautiously, but Sima seemed unconcerned. "Sima, you're not making any sense, love. What do you mean this place is cursed?"

Sima shook her head as she continued sharpening her knife. "Ajogun. Demons. Dark spirits. Dark spirits in the Ase. Infect you. Possess you. Own you. Control you. Make you Ajogun. Make us ajogun. We are ajogun. The ajogun is in us. The Ase is in us. Dark spirits are in us."

Tiwa put a gentle hand on her cousin's arm. "It's okay Sima. We can go. You and me, we can go tog—"

"This is all your fault!" Sima screamed. "I saved you. I protected you and you have cursed me!"

Tiwa recoiled. "I didn't mean to. I was just trying to do my duty and—"

"You failed! You lost the kingdom. I can't go home. My contacts have disavowed me. I'm stuck here with the Ase. I'm stuck here with Ajogun."

"We can leave. I will give myself up to Jakuta. We can leave and you can go back."

She rubbed Sima's back, wanting so much to hold her like she had done on the floor of the ship. But Sima swiped at her, slicing a thin red line into her forearm.

"I can't go back!" Even as Sima shouted, there was pleading in her eyes. "You cursed me. You cursed me.

You're the ajogun. You cursed me, cursed me, cursed, I'm cursed, you cursed me, cursed me, cursed..."

CHAPTER 21

After that haunting night in the shuttle, Tiwa gave Sima her space. The nightmares hadn't improved. Now in the absence of her friend, Tiwa found herself growing rude.

Tiwa stormed down the narrow dirt path, hauling water from the well to the field. She wasn't sure if it was the water or the fatigue but was certain she was developing a hunch. The weight of it all bore down on her and she tripped over a villager kneeling in the middle of the road. Her water buckets sloshed, throwing off her balance, drenching herself as she fell.

"Are you blind?" Tiwa spat. "What kind of fool stands in the middle of the road staring at weeds? You worthless, brainless savage!"

The villager looked at her, looked through her. What was she looking at?

"What are you looking at?"

Unfazed by the outburst, the young woman said, "apologies, my queen." Instead of retaliating, she picked the flower she had been admiring and placed it in Tiwa's hair.

Tiwa stared, her fury momentarily interrupted by confusion. "You think a flower is going to--"

Then wordlessly the young woman grabbed Tiwa's buckets and ran back down the path toward the well. Minutes later, the villager had returned, the buckets now full of fresh water. "Here," she said simply. "And peace be upon you, my queen."

Tiwa took the bucket, her fingers trembling, her anger replaced with shame. "Thank you," she muttered, her voice barely audible. The villager smiled and continued on her way. Somehow that flower felt heavier than anything she'd carried all day.

Tiwa wasn't sure if she was truly a demon or if Alkebulan was hell; either way she knew she had to go. Again, she left her bed, but this time before the nightmares had a chance to assault her.

"Where are you off to this time?" Abi asked.

"I have to check on something." she lied.

"More dreams?"

"Not tonight."

"Because you are not sleeping or because you have been cured?"

Cured?

"I have to go."

This time, she was fully dressed and ready for anything. This time, Tiwa approached her shuttle. This time, the lights were off.

Good.

"Nice evening for a stroll."

Tiwa shrieked and leapt into the air. She fumbled for her knife which clattered to the ground. Then she froze in a sort of half stooped crouch.

"Bankole?"

The retired Umantyi smiled, his eyes full of warmth and knowing. "Running away now, are we, child?"

Tiwa glared at him. "I don't belong here. I'm done with this place--these people. I'm sick of farming and folk tales--magic and ancestors and spirits. I need to live. I need to help the Zadzisai. I need to stop the Doje. I can't do that from here."

Bankole shook his head. "Did you know your mother was born here."

"What are you talking about? She was born on Baja."

"Your parents met on Baja, but Bahati was born here. She was Onyilogwu as you are now."

"That can't be. My father would have--"

Bankole laughed. "Your father was a very skilled liar. Bahati was the only one who knew every time. Come, walk with me."

The two strolled through the black night in silence for a time, letting the moonlight guide them.

"It is said, the Onyilogwu were once called the Ariotele. The Ariotele were like any tribe in the Isowo Federation. Seeking their fortune, they sent a fleet to the Asaaju system which at the time was said to be cursed."

"At the time?"

Bankole produced an apple and handed it to Tiwa, "eat this, child. It will nourish your belly and shut you up while I nourish your mind."

Tiwa took a bite with a loud snap.

"The Ase, it was called, this curse. When the Ariotele entered Alkebulan's atmosphere, their ship's navigation failed, and they crashed. The Ariotele were strong. They had more than ten thousand tribesmen and sought to claim this world. But the land was harsh. While technically habitable, the planet was a nightmare. Some continents were barren deserts, others frozen tundra. Others still were thick jungles filled with deadly creatures."

"This is how the settling of a new planet has always been. Our technology —"

"Your technology is nothing," Bankole snapped. "Nothing." He shook his head. "Nothing compared to the Ase."

Tiwa rolled her eyes.

Bankole stopped and faced her. "A crew of ten thousand, half was a battalion of soldiers. All reduced to one-hundred and fifty."

"Why didn't they signal for help?"

"The Ase would not let them leave."

A shudder went up Tiwa's spine.

"There was one among them. An engineer. He was unaffected by the Ase. He was egungun. He taught the others to be egungun. Those who would listen. And those who listened survived. The Onyilogwu survived."

"It was a virus. He had some immunity."

Bankole shook his head again. "The way of life here is hard. This is why Onyilogwu travel as youths. They see what life is like on other worlds. Some return, some don't. Your mother intended to return," he smiled and continued walking.

"But she met my father."

"The Ase is a living magic. The Ase rewards egungun, those who honor the ancestors and walk with wisdom. The Ase punishes ajogun, those who are guided by greed and fear and anger. The Ase tests you, child. Day and night and night and day. Listen and the Ase will speak."

CHAPTER 22

Again, Tiwa awoke from her father's death, her heart racing as his heart stopped. The Ase curses ajogun. The Ase blesses egungun. She almost laughed at Bankole's cryptic words. The universe was governed by empirical laws, it was rational, logical, practical. There were problems and there were solutions. You were strong or you were weak. You mitigated threats and seized opportunities. The very idea of magic influencing her fate seemed absurd, a distraction from the real issues at hand. The Doje. The Zadzisai. Isaac, Tabari, Kazim. That stupid pop song Kazim had whistled when he sent her to her cage.

Her body tensed and she clenched her fists. She needed answers. Something was going on. Bankole knew it. Abi knew it. She turned to see her husband had gone. She touched his side of the bed, feeling its warmth. How could he sleep like a baby each night? Why was he so good to her? The corner of her mouth turned up, slightly.

"The Ase blesses egungun."

Later that day, as the sun rose high overhead, Tiwa and the villagers worked the fields. Who were these people? The Onyilogwu started the day with silence, but always ended with song. That had been her only comfort throughout the grueling days. But now she listened closer.

It started with a hum. It was rarely the same person, rarely the same tune, but someone always started. This morning it was her. Not because she wanted to, but she couldn't help it. She hummed that stupid pop song, then everyone sang along.

Tiwa couldn't tell if she wanted to laugh or cry. She immediately stopped, but the song had spread like fire. They sang it as they harvested. They sang it as they milled. Women sang it as they sewed. Men sang it as they built. The women stopped to cheer the men who raised a roof with pulleys. They spoke kindly and clapped along. It was like telepathy.

These people didn't just believe in the Ase, they let it guide their lives. They slept in peace every single night. They were all so damned polite.

She railed against the idea of surrendering to anything. She refused to bend the knee to superstitious bunk. But then she saw Sima's hut, removed from all the rest. She didn't want to share her fate, or that of the ninety-nine of one hundred Ariotele who all went mad and died.

In that moment, standing on the field while the On-yilogwu celebrated, she stood alone and did not speak. She closed her eyes and immediately felt very stupid. Then the wind blew. She felt the air rush past her and the heat of the sun seemed to lessen. The sound of the villagers faded, and she started to feel an impression. Like a pressure, like a force, like water through a sieve. It flowed from head to toe and through her fingertips. She swayed there in the breeze and in her mind's eye saw a tree of glass, an emerald seed, and heard a plover's call.

When she opened her eyes, she found everyone had stopped. They looked at her in unison for a moment, some smiling with their mouths, all smiling with their eyes. Then just as suddenly as the moment had come, the commotion resumed, and they all went back to work.

Over the next several weeks, Tiwa immersed herself in the Onyilogwu way. She began to join in the villagers' daily rituals. She offered prayers to the ancestors and honored the spirits of the land. She still didn't believe in gods and Ase, but she participated because they did. The young woman who had given her the flower, taught her the importance of balance in all things. We are animals, we are humans, we are spirits. We tend the fields for our animal nature. We collaborate for our human self. We serve and sacrifice for our spirit. What at first felt like a charade became a need, became a drive.

She helped her sisters, brothers, aunties, and uncles with great care. Not from obligation, but awareness and with great pride. Her anger melted all away, her hate nowhere in sight. And then she made love to Abi, and she slept all through the night.

CHAPTER 23

Alkebulan turned, seasons passed, and Tiwa found her rhythm. To her surprise, she loved to cook, making lunch for Abi before work. Instead of buzzing, she often sang, she found she liked her voice. Her mind grew calm, her body firm, her hands both quick and rough. Though strong before, she realized that she wasn't very tough. This dark and stormy world where caves hid danger deep within. The hardships didn't seem so hard when everyone pitched in.

She was a queen, but unlike before, she belonged in every meeting. They were curious about their new queen and so she hosted an event. Everyone came. The capital village came in person, and they set up a livestream. She would later learn that more than ten million people attended. By Zadzisai standards that was a raindrop in river, but there only fifteen million Onyilogwu.

Her friends pushed her onto the stage of the local community center, demanding that she speak. She was nervous and a little dizzy. This was her first formal address. The literal world was watching. Thinking it best to avoid anything too maudlin about how she came to their planet, she decided to tell a story.

"I have very few memories of my mother. I only recently learned she was Onyilogwu."

The crowd whistled a two-note bird call, as that was their way. They wore no sigils like the other Federation tribes. They whistled to one another in passing. They whistled or kissed, cheek to cheek.

"Bahati," she said, and her stomach swooned. She closed her eyes to calm her nerves and pictured the tree of glass. "We were in the garden of my family's estate. Father was away on business and so we decided to have a picnic. The blanket was set with potato salad, barbeque chicken and blackberry pie. I'm not going to lie, I would kill for some blackberry pie, right now."

The crowd laughed. "I will make it for you!" Someone shouted.

"We had just begun to eat when a fly started buzzing around my food. My mother told me to let it be, but of course, I did not listen. I swatted at it and felt satisfied to connect. Take that you stupid fly, I thought. But it did not die. It stung me. I had never felt a pain like this before. And my pain was just beginning. You see that fly was not a fly. It was a hornet. We had set our picnic beneath his nest and soon his brothers came to defend his honor."

Everyone gasped.

"Oh, you have no idea. I was terrified. They swarmed out of that nest like demons from the darkest cave. They all came rushing for me and they began to sting me all over."

"What did you do?" Someone called.

"I listened."

Whistles sounded from the gathered crowd and Tiwa's eyes welled up. Though she felt faint at the memory, she continued.

"My mother whistled as you do now. She whistled and then she sang. She walked through the cloud of yellow jackets like they were little more than vapor. She walked right up to me and scooped me into her arms. Then as if by some magic, the hornets let me be. I always wondered how she could be so beloved by all of man and nature. But I think you know."

More whistles.

"Now, after being among you all, I know it was the As—"

Tiwa's gut lurched and she ran from the stage to vomit. There was no word for the embarrassment she felt. Though many knocks came by her door, she hid from her party, indignant. But when the doctor looked at her, he told her she was pregnant.

Although Tiwa and Abi had discussed having a child someday, she hadn't expected it to happen so soon. But when he found out, Abi's typically happy face practically glowed. Damn that man, his optimism was infectious.

Abi whistled his bird call and hoisted Tiwa into the air. "Today is a glorious day!" He set her down. "I am sorry about your speech. I wish I could have met your mother. She would no doubt be very proud."

Tiwa wiped the water from her cheeks and nodded. Abi had gone before the crowd and announced they would have a new heir. Tiwa had to admit, for a bunch of backwater bumpkins, the Onyilogwu knew how to party. Only, the party felt incomplete.

Using her old sneaking skills, Tiwa made a surreptitious exit. The speakers boomed from the community center and the commotion from partygoers outside. But there was no party without her savior, her cousin, her best friend in all the universe.

The celebratory sounds faded to soft drumbeats as Tiwa approached Sima hut.

She found Sima pacing in front of her hut, having a conversation with herself. "It is done, it is done. You did it. It's done. You know you shouldn't have. It will make things worse for Zibi. I know, but I can't stay here any longer. This is worse than — "

The stream of consciousness stopped, and Sima turned to her cousin. Her eyes shifted in all directions, as if watching an invisible fly. The sight was unnerving. Sima had always been so composed and disciplined, so full of laughter and cheer. Now she looked like a vagabond, skin barely containing her bones.

She needed this. Sima had saved her so many times, Tiwa desperately wanted to return the favor.

She had tried and failed in the shuttle, but now she came bearing hope.

Sima's mouth twisted as if uncertain whether to display fear, relief, or suspicion. "You came. Good. Good. Good, good, good. I have been making plans, Zibi," Sima said, her voice laced with conspiracy.

Tiwa reached out to embrace her friend and Sima barreled into her embrace. She clung to Tiwa like a drowning man at sea. Wrapping her arms around her too thin body, Tiwa gave a gentle squeeze, afraid she might hurt the woman.

Then just as suddenly as she had grabbed her, Sima let go. "We can leave this cursed place. I have made it so. We can leave this place soon. So soon. We can leave. We can leave. We can go."

"What are you talking about? I will talk to Abi, you can go if you like, but this is my home now. These are my people. I am Onyilogwu."

Sima shook her head so fiercely, Tiwa thought it might come off. "I've saved us," she said, smiling with yellowing teeth. "I've struck a deal with the Doje. They will be here in three days' time."

CHAPTER 24

Tiwa itched like curses under her skin.

"Legend said Yamandulo sorcerers commanded undead armies," said Sima, her voice hollow and not fully her own. "These necromancers would whisper a curse onto the wind. The curse wind would find its target and possess him."

Tiwa took an involuntary step back. "You made a deal with the Doje?"

Sima's eyes had darted around scanning for eavesdroppers, but now they seemed lucid and clear. "I have kept you alive this long, haven't I? Trust..." The word lingered in the space between them. "...I am doing what is best for everyone."

Who was this woman? Where had her cousin gone?

"Sima, listen to me," said Tiwa, "Don't you re-member what happened to Bankole's home? They'll kill us the moment they arrive."

The corners of her mouth drooped, and her lower lip lifted. A crack. Sima was still inside. Tiwa reached for her hand and placed it on her belly.

"Let's talk to the elders. I am going to have a child. We will find a way."

Sima pressed her palms against her eyes. Then she shook her head and laughed. She laughed through her tears as her voice cracked.

"It really makes no difference."

Sima reversed her grip and grabbed onto Tiwa's wrist. The woman's hand was a vice.

"You're my only way out. I did it for both of us. I get to live; you get to escape the nightmares."

"Killing me was your part of the deal."

Before Tiwa could react, Sima lunged at her, dag-ger flashing in the low light. Tiwa barely dodged, the blade grazing her arm. Pain shot through her, but she gritted her teeth. Now she would have matching scars.

"You don't have to do this."

But Sima struck again, and this time, Tiwa wasn't fast enough. Sima's knee drove into her stomach, knocking the wind out of her and sending her sprawl-ing to the ground. Before Tiwa could recover, Sima was on top of her with cold steel pressed against her throat.

Tiwa struggled, her strength waning as Sima's weight bore down on her. She saw the tree of glass and stopped struggling. "I'm sorry I couldn't save you."

Then as she spoke, a warmth blossomed in her chest. It spread through her limbs and her skin began to glow. Soft, radiant blue light pulsed with the rhythm of her heartbeat. Sima's eyes widened, her madness replaced by fear. With a surge of strength, Tiwa grabbed Sima's wrists and threw her off with a massive burst of force.

Sima flew across the room, her back slamming into the wall of the hut then falling to the dirt below. The dagger she still clutched was driven deep into her own abdomen. Sima's breath hitched, and blood bloomed on her tunic.

Tiwa found her feet, body still glowing faintly as she stared at her friend.

Sima shuddered, but as she convulsed, she kept trying to speak. "Y-y-y, k-k-k, l-l-lion." She gasped. "Ancient. Time. You'd kill the lion."

CHAPTER 25

Tiwa never bothered to sit as the Onyilogwu leaders filed into the chamber of elders. She swept her eyes over the room while the others wiped the sleep from their eyes.

"Respected elders," she began, "the time for peace is over. The Doje are coming."

Silence filled the chamber.

"Jakuta and his tribe of snakes are intent on swallowing the Isowo Federation whole. They have ignored Alkebulan up to this point because we are small and, in their eyes, insignificant. But now, because of me, the Doje are coming."

"Don't you think you're being a little dramatic?" Said an older woman.

"No. I watched them destroy Bankole's planet without so much as a warning. If we wait for them to strike, we're as good as dead."

Another man cleared his throat. "Why three days? They could be here in one jump from their nearest port. Why wait?"

"Arrogance. It's all in the police report. Jakuta weaponized my cousin Sima against me. He gave her three days to kill me, and she failed on the first day. Which is why we must capitalize on the advantage and rally our forces now."

Tiwa pulled up a map of the planet. "We would need to fortify these areas as critical during the siege. That is what we will do tonight. Tomorrow, we launch a preemptive strike at Jakuta's host. There is no guarantee he will wait the full three days. Our only chance is to cut off the head of the snake."

Where she expected determination in the council's eyes, instead she saw polite nonchalance. The elders, some ancient, all seasoned in their wisdom, exchanged almost humorous glances.

"I don't understand the joke." Tiwa said. "Would someone care to fill me in?"

"Inside joke," said a middle-aged man.

"Queen Tiwa," said the older woman, "we understand your concern, but war is not our way. We will defend ourselves if the Doje come, but we will not go to war."

CHAPTER 26

Tiwa felt her grip beginning to slip. The elders were wise, yes, but their wisdom was forged in a different time. The Doje were not like the enemies of old; they were ruthless conquerors who left no survivors. "Can't you see? You're being naïve!" she nearly shouted her desperation. "We can't win this battle with magic and tradition alone. If we don't strike first, there will be no Onyilogwu left for the Ase to protect!"

She stormed out of the chamber and Abi raced after her.

Tiwa wheeled on him in the corridor. "Why didn't you have my back in there?"

"We all admire your passion for our people."

"You agree with them!" She shook her head as if slapped by the revelation. The corridor fell silent. She had anticipated resistance, but not this stubborn passivity, not from Abi.

"Yes." he said. "Onyilogwu are immune to dark magic. We do not go to war."

Her anger boiled over into bitterness as she realized the futility of further argument. How could they be so blind? She could feel the war drums in the distance, hear Jakuta's laughter in the back of her mind.

"Fine. Then I will find another way to defend us, with or without your support."

As soon as she reached the privacy of her quarters, Tiwa contacted the mercenary admiral she had hired to defend the Agu. "War is coming. I need every ship, firearm, and blade your company can muster, and I need them in Alkebulan by morning."

"I had a feeling I'd be hearing from you again, ma'am. Given the severity of the mission, this won't be cheap." Said the admiral, rough voice belying his smooth demeanor.

Tiwa buzzed her lips. "Hold back the Doje, while I get an assassin aboard his ship. After that, you will have all the spoils you can handle."

The admiral chuckled, a dark sound that made her skin itch. "Consider it done."

Eshu had been whispering schemes into her ear again. She knew how to reclaim the Zadzisai lands. She would kill Jakuta and make Alkebulan the capital of the Isowo Federation.

CHAPTER 27

Returning home in the early morning hours, she found Abi waiting for her with tea. The Doje were closing in and there was no time left for diplomacy. They needed to secure the safety of the king and royal family. Yet, here was the king, waiting up like a father on prom night.

"Abi, listen to me. I think you may be in shock. It's okay. I have prepared for these things. That is how I survived. That is how we will survive."

Abi stared blankly at her.

"Since the elders have refused to prepare for war, I've summoned a mercenary fleet. They cannot contend with the Doje, only stall their main host while I slip an assassin inside Jakuta's ship. You need to stay with me where it is safe. Safe for you safe for our child. Safe for us all until the difficult work is done."

"Tiwa," Abi said, sitting down the cup of tea. "What do you know of the Umantyi?"

Umantyi? The judges?

"What have they to do with any of this?"

"The Umantyi are the last remnants of the Ancient Yamandulo. They left us a free society. They left us the ability to choose how to live our lives. The Yamandulo believed in truth and promises. That is why the Umantyi bless contracts. The Yamandulo believed your word was sacred."

"I understand what you're saying," Tiwa began. "I understand you believe this, but you have to trust me. You have not seen politics on this scale, but I have trained my entire life for this. Let me handle it."

Abi took Tiwa's hand in his own. "The Umantyi have grown corrupt. The Isowo Federation is unbalanced. We swing from tribalism to tyranny, anarchy to monopoly. The Umantyi were created to keep the pendulum swinging. But they are not the only structures the Yamandulo built."

Tiwa's grip tightened on her husband's hands. "Abi, we don't have time! The Doje could strike any moment, and I can't protect our child or our people alone. Please, just come with me. Don't make me do this on my own."

Abi smiled and kissed Tiwa on the cheek. "You're not alone, my love. We are all here for you. I promise."

CHAPTER 28

Tiwa stared at the man in disbelief. The longer she waited, the more likely she was to crack. Something was terribly wrong, here. Were these people actually cursed? Was the Ase something in the water? Abi's reassurances did nothing to quell the dread that grew like ivy in her gut.

The sky was literally about to fall, and he was drinking tea.

She couldn't listen to Abi. The elders were crazy like Sima. Everyone on this planet was crazy. Or was she the crazy one? She couldn't leave Abi, no matter what his crazy superstitious beliefs made him do.

She straddled him and pressed her lips to his. She held him with all her might and kissed him with all the passion she felt for him, for his goodness for his love.

She hugged him around his neck and whispered in his ear. "I will save us."

Then she ran. Tiwa ran as fast as her legs would carry her. She ran to see Bankole. Bankole would understand.

Tiwa burst through Bankole's door and scanned the room. The old man sat in a chair reading a tablet.

"What is wrong with you child?"

"Bankole, we have to go. I'm going to meet with the Admiral, and I need you to get Abi to safety."

Bankole scowled. "The only thing I need to do is stay black and die."

Tiwa struggled to keep the panic from her voice. "Abi wants me to wait, but I can't just sit here while the Doje destroy my home again. The elders won't listen, but I have a plan. I just need to get as many people to safety as possible before the Doje ship arrives. And I need you to help me do it."

CHAPTER 29

Bankole stared at Tiwa as if her declaration of war had been between two warring factions of action figures.

"Why are the Doje coming so soon?"

"Sima betrayed us. She's made a deal with the Doje to sell me out and..." Tiwa paused, then glanced backward toward the door. "What do you mean 'so soon'?"

"Come in and have some tea. We can—"

"Why is everyone always offering me bloody tea!?"

Bankole took a loud slurp from his mug. "It calms the nerves. Do you think this was not a possibility Ajaka had planned for?"

"And what did he expect? That Abi would protect me? The man is in shock. He can barely comprehend what is going on!"

"I seriously doubt that. He is very lucid. Too lucid for me. I find him a bit corny."

"Bankole, all I need you to do is get Abi and the elders to get the people into the shelters I've marked on this map. If you will just—"

"He won't go. None of them will."

"But why?" She pleaded.

"Because you are not yet full Onyilogwu," said Abi from the door.

"Initiation rights?"

"Initiation rights?" Tiwa cried. "You're keeping me in the dark for superstitious initiation rites?"

Then her earphone rang.

"I'm at the rendezvous location. Where are you?"

She grabbed her husband by the collar. "That's the admiral. Abi, the Doje are coming. We have to go, now. This is life and death."

Before Abi could respond, his earphone buzzed, and he took the call on speaker via his wristwatch. "Oba Abiodun," came Jakuta's smooth deep voice. "I was in the neighborhood and hoping I could stop by for tea."

Abi cocked his head at Tiwa as if to say, 'see?' "I am always happy to have a friendly neighbor over for tea."

"Good, good. I am glad you see reason. There's no need for unnecessary bloodshed."

"I could not agree more."

"Come to my ship and we will discuss this like kings."

CHAPTER 30

Tiwa's stomach churned. How could Abi be entertaining this snake's venomous offer? She seethed at the idea of her husband bowing to Jakuta.

Her frustration exploded into rage. "You're actually listening to him?" she snapped, stepping closer to Abi. "Jakuta doesn't care about peace. He'll carve up your lands and take everything from you once you surrender!"

Abi's calm gaze only fueled her anger further. "You're not seeing the bigger picture, Tiwa. If we resist, we all die. If we negotiate, we might save something."

Abi was right in one sense — they were outmatched. But how could he sacrifice everything so easily? Ajaka had fought for this marriage, to keep her safe. Abi had promised. All that talk of Umantyi and Yamandulo promises.

Before Abi could react, Tiwa snatched the phone from his ear and bolted. Abi shouted after her, but she didn't look back. Her heart pounded as she raced out of Bankole's house to see the black winged warships darkening the sky.

The Doje weren't waiting for negotiations — they were ready to strike. Why didn't they? She knew as soon as she thought it and Tiwa fell to her knees.

"Take me," she said into the jawbone mic. "Take me. Leave these people alone. Please."

Her fingers moved swiftly, calling off the mercenaries. If her people were going to survive, she needed to remove all hostility. She would go. They would live.

CHAPTER 31

Jakuta laughed. "I have everything I want, except your life. I will accept your offer."

Abi joined Tiwa where she stood in the courtyard as a Doje privateer descended from the main host. Maybe if they brought an Umantyi judge, he could bless the contract. He would bless the contract and Jakuta would spare her people. But if Abi was to be believed, the Umantyi were corrupt, and their blessings were unenforceable.

The ship's bay door opened, and a squad of soldiers exited, making way for their master. Jakuta stepped forward and drew his first breath on Alkebulan.

"Welcome," Abi said, approaching his murderous guest. "I apologize for greeting you with such meager accommodations. Had I known you were coming, I would have prepared something more grand in your honor."

Jakuta looked around at Bankole's rural countryside manor house. "Your accommodations are meager indeed. I am tempted to destroy this planet for your sake."

"Shall we go inside to discuss—"

Jakuta backhanded Abi across the mouth with his metal gauntlet.

"No!" Tiwa screamed.

"You think I'd settle for just one person? Your life is worthless. Your only real value is for marketing purposes. The spectacle of your death will incentivize the others into compliance. I will take you, and I will take the planet. I will make sure every blade of grass, every drop of water, and every living thing on Alkebulan is reduced to ash. And when this world is nothing but smears of cinder, then I will enjoy watching you die. I will revel in the knowledge that I have broken everything Ajaka has built. Everything he took from me, I will have returned with interest. The only currency I will accept for this transaction is blood."

Jakuta's words struck Tiwa like a physical blow. Her knees buckled, and she collapsed to her hands and begged. Tears welled in her eyes as she whispered, "I'm sorry, Father. I couldn't stop him. I have failed you."

The courtyard seemed surreal, as daylight tried and failed to shine from behind the Doje legions. Their forms cast long shadows between the ancient stone pillars surrounding the open space. Tiwa was seized by Jakuta's guards and despite her struggling they held her. And she was forced to watch as Jakuta rained blow after blow upon Abi.

"Weak," Jakuta said, more irritated than angry, each strike of metal on flesh, Abi gasped, a futile attempt to draw a breath.

Wet thuds echoed through the courtyard as Tiwa watched her husband get hurled around like a doll.

"I'm so tired of you people. So soft, so fragile, so afraid to seize what's right in front of you." The monster turned to Tiwa, as she fought against the guards' restraints. "You think strength is about power, but it's not just that. It's about opportunity. It's about crushing your enemies before they can even think to rise against you."

As if on cue, Abi tried to stand.

"I'll make the Federation strong. I will make a contest. No one is exempt. The strong will rule the weak." Jakuta paused, a twisted smile forming on his lips as he stomped on Abi's lower leg. With a sickening crunch Abi's bones broke and broke through his skin. He looked as though he would howl but was too exhausted to make a sound.

"And maybe," Jakuta continued. "Just maybe, one day they'll be strong enough to kill me. But I will only be killed by a worthy opponent."

Blood dripped from Abi's mouth as he collapsed onto the cold stones, but Jakuta wasn't done. He kicked Abi's side, flipping him onto his back. He knelt over the battered backwater king and raised his fist to deliver his final blow. But just as Jakuta's fist began to descend, Abi's body burst with brilliant blue light.

Jakuta was launched into the air. He froze, looking upon the fallen king, his face paled. Abi's wounds began to knit themselves back together. The protruding bones in his leg, pressing back through the skin as if on rewind. Abi stood, the cuts and bruises fading as if they were never there.

Then the sky became awash with light. Stars filled the heavens and dotting it so bright, they blotted out the darkness that the Doje fleet had made. It was as if the gods themselves had come to Abi's aid.

"What is this?" Jakuta growled, his bravado faltering as he sat up from where he had landed.

"Dry your eyes, Tiwa," said Abi's voice, only it sounded clearer, cleaner, almost as if it were many voices in one, all beamed directly into her mind. "See why we have waited."

Abi rose to his feet, his body glowing with energy. It seemed to pulse, it seemed alive, but how? How could this be? Jakuta rolled onto his knuckles and his mech suit powered up. The monster lunged at Abi, but unconcerned as ever, her husband evaded the blow. He stepped at the right moment. Jakuta looked so slow. But they were moving fast, the Doje's suit enhanced his strength. He tried to stomp and broke the stone, but they weren't on the same wavelength. No matter how many times Jakuta swung, his blows would never land. Abi danced, then he blew a kiss to Tiwa with his glowing hand.

"You're nothing!" Jakuta roared, his voice cracking. "Shoot him!" He called out to his soldiers, "Kill him now!"

The soldiers fired, their weapons hot, but the bullets did not land. They hit an invisible shield, that turned the tungsten to sand. Panic flared in Jakuta's eyes as he barked the order to flee. But before they could respond, Abi made his decree.

"I am Oba Abiodun," Abi's voice echoed across the courtyard, and in Tiwa's earphone. "I am Oba Abiodun, king of the Onyilogwu and chief Umantyi Judge. Today, I have witnessed the Doje's crimes and justice will be served."

Jakuta's face fell as a holographic map of the solar system appeared before Alkebulan's king. It appeared like the mural on the wall of the chamber of elders, a minefield across the galaxy. The Yamandulo fleet came alive. Abi raised his hands, and Tiwa couldn't tell if it was smoke or fire or mist that rose from her husband's skin. He pointed to the Doje ships and like a deadly moving constellation, they surrounded Jakuta's fleet.

"All Doje will be arrested and made to stand trial for their crimes against the Isowo Federation. Any who resist shall be judged." Then he turned his glowing eyes to Jakuta, his expression hardening. "Oba Jakuta, you have brought nothing but shame and death upon so many people. Thus, by the power vested in me, I sentence you to death."

"Fire!" Jakuta screamed, and madness gripped his voice.

The Doje ships entered battle stance but would not get their chance. The holomap displayed their moves and made the phalanx dance. Yamandulo snuffed the Doje fleet like moths to a bonfire. Tiwa felt concussion waves that shook the ground entire. The Doje forces were no more, wiped out just like a stain. Jakuta watched the sky ignite, he was all that remained.

Still glowing with the power of the Ase, Abi knelt. He held Jakuta's hand, the warlord cried. Tiwa's heart felt. Jakuta was her foe, but what a waste for him to die. But Abi touched Jakuta's brow, and the light went from his eyes.

CHAPTER 32

Watching the life drain from her enemy, Tiwa's heart swelled with sorrow. Her eyes burned, her breath caught, and though the Doje soldiers released her, she felt the bars of a new cage.

Power radiated off Abi's skin like a fiery mist. Those superstitious stories, those folk tales to frighten children. They were real. They were real and they stood right in front of her. They burned the sky above her. Pieces of broken ships rained fire as they fell through the atmosphere. But Abi's hologram detected them as red dots which he deftly snuffed out like a video game. She watched overhead as the meteors should have extincted the planet. But they were shot down and contained by drones that moved at hyper speeds. They moved at the speed of Abi's thought.

She ran toward her husband, but instead of leaping into his arms, she drew up short. While undeniably awe-inspiring, Tiwa felt the grip of terror. If he can kill so effortlessly, what else is he capable of?

She tried to move, but her feet faltered. Threat neutralized, Abi turned his gaze to Tiwa, the Ase still glowing within them.

"Abi…" she whispered, voice trembling, "is that you?"

Standing in the middle of Bankole's broken courtyard, surrounded by the remnants of battle, Tiwa felt torn between her love for Abi and the fear of what he had become. His generosity had become her anchor on this planet. His kindness a lighthouse in the dark, but now, that intensity became a weight of judgment.

Her husband was not only the Chief Judge of the Umantyi, he held the power of the Ase. And with that power, he could easily conquer the entire Isowo Federation. This power, the Ase, this divine authority, could be used against her and she would have no defense.

She had lived her life as an opportunist, plotting, posturing, positioning for maximum advantage. As Chief Judge, he had the authority to pass judgment not just on her, but on her father's legacy as well. How could she truly surrender now, knowing what she stood to lose?

Abi took a step forward and Tiwa took a step back.

If she surrendered to her love, she would be submitting to whatever sentence he deemed just.

Abi waited.

Why?

What was he waiting for?

Then she saw the glass tree in her mind's eye, and it all became clear. If she allowed her fear to take over, it would corrupt her. She would become like Sima and Jakuta.

Her heart beat faster and she ran with it. She rushed into Abi's arms and kissed him.

"Don't you ever scare me like that again!"

Abi smiled. "You asked me to help you bring justice to your enemies. I have done so, but I have not yet fulfilled my promise."

Abi took Tiwa by the hand. "Bankole," he called to the old man standing outside of the doorway. "Please offer these Doje soldiers some tea while they wait for the police."

The soldiers bowed and murmured their thanks as Abi and Tiwa strolled past.

"Abi, what just happened?" Tiwa asked. "Why didn't you tell me you commanded the Yamandulo phalanx?"

Abi sighed. "I tried to explain this to you many times. But you would not listen. You are so stubborn. You would ask a question, then run away every time I tried to answer you."

"You kept offering me tea while the world was literally on fire."

The king clicked his tongue. "I offered you tea first. The fire came later."

She punched his arm.

"Would you like to know now?"

Tiwa nodded.

"Firstly, I could not tell you the whole of it. As Onyilogwu, you are allowed to learn of the Ase as a force. As my queen, you are entitled to know more, but not all. You see, the Umantyi are secret society. If I told you all our secrets, then we would not be a very secret society, now, would we?" He smiled. "That is the problem. All Umantyi judges were meant to come to Alkebulan to be trained. The process is very grueling. The Ase judges them and they either become egungun or die."

"That's a rather severe hazing ritual." said Tiwa.

"Yes. Yes, it is. It must be. Because as judges they can command the Yamandulo phalanx to enforce contracts. But when they go back into the world, they will be tempted."

"So how did they become corrupt?"

"They fractionated. A growing number of Umantyi could not stand the life of an egungun. They refused to return to Alkebulan and overthrew the true Umantyi."

"That is why the Yamandulo fleet has been dormant despite corrupt contracts."

"Yes. And that is why Jakuta was able to murder your father in an Umantyi courthouse with impunity."

Tiwa released Abi's hand. "You knew he was going to die."

"We knew it was a possibility. So, in preparation for his death, he came here for penance. Ajaka had many demons, but he was strong. Like Bahati, like you. He became egungun and returned to the world to face Jakuta and judgment for his crimes."

She remembered her father's last words. "Be good, for you are loved."

"His last words were for his enemy because he knew Jakuta needed a reason to change. And he knew you would eventually find your way. Besides, you can speak to your parents any time you want. The Ase holds their memories in the Onyilogwu hive mind."

"Really?"

"Oh yes. When we get home, I will show you how."

This was all too much.

"So, what is the Ase?" Tiwa asked. The question had been burning a hole in her tongue.

"Nanites."

"Seriously?"

"Mostly. They are not purely mechanical. They are like artificial intelligence made from configurable energy structures. The physics is quite profound."

"They're not magic?"

"Of course they are. A great Yamandulo once said, any technology sufficiently advanced is indistinguishable from magic. But at its core, the Ase is a security system. Instead of a retinal scan, it assesses your honor."

"So, anyone with the prerequisite character can wield the power?"

"Yes. Honor is not like life and death. It cannot be given nor taken away. It must be chosen. It must be earned. Choose it or don't. Pay for it, or don't. And if the price is your life, and you have chosen to pay for it, then even if you have lived as the most wicked of vermin– you cannot erase the past–but you can pay the price and you can die with honor. That is the teaching of the Ase. That is what it means to be egungun. If you are egungun, you will not use it for anything other than it's intended purpose. Why do you think we hold no other estates?"

Then Tiwa stopped and turned to face her husband. She kissed him and said, "We have everything we need, right here."

UMANTYI'S NOTES

The Isowo Federation is a conglomeration of 13 solar systems with 50 habitable planets governed by the Umantyi Interplanetary Estate Authority. These systems and planets are owned and controlled by 11 tribes.

The Zadzisai and Doje are the two dominant tribes in the federation. While the Zadzisai have alliances with the Jelani, Igwe, and Furaha tribes, the Doje have alliances with the Mmeremikwu and Nwadike. The Agu, Oyawale, Keita, and Onyilogwu are all independent tribes.

Of collectives of dominant tribes, the Zadzisai own 22 worlds, the Doje own 19, the independent tribes own 9 worlds, and of those 9 worlds, the Onyilogwu own only 1. The Onyilogwu, however, are unique because their one world, Alkebulan, is the most remote in the federation and exists in a solar system all its own.

AGU

A·gu • /a.gu/ • AH-goo
STRENGTH IN SILENCE

CULTURE

The Agu were once the greatest of all Yamondulo tribes, possessing the first and only monopoly in the Isowo Federation. Though fierce warriors and merchants, they grew entitled and failed to adapt to the changing politics and marketplace. Their empire was dismantled by the technologically superior Igwe and they never recovered.

TRADITIONS

TIGER WARRIORS

An elite order of warriors who defend the weak and uphold a strict moral code set down by their ancestor spirits.

THE STAR CEREMONY

A ritual honoring fallen ancestors where rockets containing dyed precious minerals are shot into space and detonated. Then like fireworks they rain wealth down upon the Agu people.

KEEPER OF GLORY

Keepers are elder historians charged with ensuring the culture endures. Each year, there is a Recitation of Glory, where every Agu attends a gathering to hear a Keeper recite the oral history of the tribe.

DOJE

Do·je • /dɔ.dʒe/ • DOH-jay

WE HUNT, WE EAT, WE GROW

CULTURE

The Doje are an expansionist and hierarchical people, willing to survive at all costs. Descended from fallen Yamondulo aristocrats, they value power, control, and loyalty to their kin. Their society is ruled by a chief and his council of warlords, who enforce strict governance and personal fealty.

TRADITIONS

NIGHT OF VENOM

A brutal initiation where all adults prove their fortitude and endurance by being injected with snake venom and surviving from dusk till dawn without medical aid.

BLOOD OATHS

Fealty is sworn in blood, and betrayal is punishable by exile or death.

DIVINE KINGSHIP

Following a series of trials, the Oba is bles-sed by the serpent god Apohpus and granted spiritual authority over the tribe.

FURAHA

Fu·ra·ha • /fu.ra.ha/ • foo-RAH-hah

PURPOSE, PEACE, PROSPERITY

CULTURE

The Furaha are mediators and bridge-builders, valuing tolerance and pragmatism. Their society is open to all, and they pride themselves on their ability to balance differing viewpoints without conflict. Their compassion, however, is frequently their undoing as they rely too heavily on technology for security. Thus, they often lose in battle to more militarily savvy tribes.

TRADITIONS

KITH PACTS

A tradition where families formally adopt outsiders as kin.

MISSIONARY'S OATH

Diplomats undergo a ritual where they swear an oath to respect and preserve each culture they encounter.

SACRED GARDENS

Communal spaces in every Furaha municipality dedicated to reflection on life's mysteries.

IGWE

I·gwe • /i.gʷe/ • EE-gway

BUILD IT BETTER

CULTURE

The Igwe are intellectuals and reformers, believing in the power of education and science. Descended from Yamondulo scientists, they see knowledge as sacred and work to create a just, ordered society. Despite their enthusiasm for technological advancement, their reason often gives way to their pride. They ruled the Isowo Federation for a century as a near monopoly before being outmaneuvered by Zadzisai cunning.

TRADITIONS

MASTER SCHOLARS

Governance is determined by those who prove intellectual merit. Their king is either the wisest among them or the one who has produced the most popular literature.

THE GREAT DEBATE

In elections, leaders argue policy before the people in massive stadiums with referees like sports matches. Every Igwe Oba has been crowned debate champion at least once.

ORACLOMETRY

Their religion is a sort of technopuritanism whereby the Igwe use artificial intelligence for divination.

JELANI

Je·la·ni • /dʒɛ.lɑː.ni/ • jeh-LAH-nee

SEEK THE VALUE

CULTURE

The Jelani are an industrious people, believing that hard work is the key to a prosperous future. Descended from Yamondulo craftsmen, they have a deep respect for labor, family, and self-sufficiency. They form tight-knit communities, built around extended families and local trade networks. With such large family ties, Jelani are known for dueling with status rather than arms. In extreme circumstances they are know to throw a lavish bankruptcy party and commit suicide rather than accepting charity.

TRADITIONS

CHAIN GANGS

Youthful work crews that build homes, roads, and irrigation systems as a rite of passage before being allowed more profitable work.

THE HARVEST FESTIVAL

A major religious celebration honoring diligence and community success.

FERVOR

Their faith emphasizes both divine guidance and personal effort to shape one's destiny.

KEITA

Kei·ta • /keɪ.ta/ • KAY-tah

WORD IS BOND

CULTURE

The Keita are cosmopolitan merchants and traders, valuing inter-tribal relationships and free enterprise. Like the Oyawale, they embrace innovation and multiculturalism, but elevate commerce over justice. Their brutal draconian laws act as a deterrent to injustice, thus making the Keita the most trustworthy bankers and lawyers in the entire Isowo Federation.

TRADITIONS

THE UNBROKEN CONTRACT

Any Keita unable to fulfill a contract may invoke the Unbroken Contract to be insured by the wealthiest of the tribe. But, any who invoke it are publicly tortured to their degree of negligence.

FESTIVAL OF TONGUES

A unique celebration where each tribe is celebrated. It is very common for all eleven tribes to participate in this Keita event regardless of what world they live on.

THE TALENT TRIALS

Keita religious leaders oversee trade guilds, seeing commerce as divine. All Keita are appraised by the guild priest and given a sum of chits and a week to multiply their talents.

MMEREMIKWU

Mme·re·mi·kwu • /mːɛ.rɛ.mi.kwu/ • M-MEH-reh-MEE-kwu

DEATH BRINGS LIFE

CULTURE

A fiercely independent people, the Mmeremikwu descend from settlers who rejected centralized power. They are survivalists, valuing personal freedom and self-reliance above all. While they respect tradition, they reject excessive hierarchy, seeing government as a necessary evil at best. Any and all alliances are temporary.

TRADITIONS

CLAN COUNCILS

Leadership is decentralized, with small, tight-knit families governing themselves.

THE GREAT FEAST

A celebration of resilience, featuring boasts, feasts, and a battle royale of champions from each house, no matter how lowly.

SACRED SMITHS

Their religious leaders are all engineers who specialize in weaponsmithing. Their ability to kill small and large game with any weapon is seen as both a practical and spiritual duty.

NWADIKE

Nwa·di·ke • /ɲwa.di.kɛ/ • NWAH-dee-kay

WE MOVE AS ONE

CULTURE

The Nwadike are a diplomatic and cooperative people, descended from settlers who prioritized consensus and accommodation. They see unity as the highest good, valuing relationships and careful negotiation over conflict. Their society is built around Elders' Circles, where all voices are heard before major decisions are made. This attitude makes them susceptible to conquest with weak leadership, but with strong leaders, they become political dynamos.

TRADITIONS

FOX FIGHTS

A ritual where major disputes are settled through long-form rigorous debates, creating a sport-like spectacle, lasting weeks or months at a time.

THE SILENT MARCH

A form of protest that allows grievances to be expressed without discord. These marches grind commerce to a halt forcing the government to respond.

QUEST OF IWA

A spiritual pilgrimage where young adults travel alone through the Iwa Desert, guided only by their chosen ancestor spirit.

ONYILOGWU

On·yi·log·wu • /ɔɲ.jɪ.lɔg.wu/ • OHN-yee-LOHG-woo

WE SERVE

CULTURE

On the surface, the Onyilogwu are a quiet and unassuming people, limited in their political influence. Underneath, they are a highly advanced aristocratic society, descended from the Yamondulo courts that created the Isowo Federation. They uphold a rigid social hierarchy, where duty, honor, and sacrifice define one's place in the world. Leadership is seen as both a privilege and a burden, with elders and rulers protecting their people with wisdom and fairness or they are taken by the Ase.

TRADITIONS

JUDICIAL NOBILITY

Public service is a mark of honor, with elite houses exposed to massive physical and mental hardship in preparation to protect their people.

THE ASE

A strict mystical system of morality in service of the preservation of the human race.

UMANTYI JUDGES

A secret society who presides over contracts through the will of the Ase and the written rule of Yamondulo Law.

OYAWALE

O·ya·wa·le • /ɔ.ja.wa.lɛ/ • OH-yah-WAH-lay

JUSTICE FOR ALL

CULTURE

The Oyawale are progressives, dedicated to justice, planetary preservation, and cultural diversity. Their society is vibrant, artistic, and deeply engaged in political philosophy. Despite their outward reputation for peace, they are adept propagandists. Their primary means of expansion is to provoke a weaker enemy as justification for crusading and conquering their territory.

TRADITIONS

THE CLEANSING FIRE

Citizens hold massive rallies with enormous floats of their enemies they follow through the streets. At the Hall of Justice the floats are burned in bonfires so massive they can be seen from space.

RIVERS OF REBIRTH

River rites to honor water as the source of life and renewal. They drink from and bathe in the river to be cleansed of impurities and are reborn with every other Oyawale.

ORISHA STEWARDS

Veneration of the Orisha spirits on each planet, thanking them for their environmental stewardship and favor.

ZADZISAI

Zad·zi·sai • /zad.zi.saɪ/ • ZAH-jee-sigh

PROTECT THE CORE

CULTURE

The Zadzisai are a people forged by the harsh frontier and believe in opportunity above almost all else. They are resourceful, pragmatic, and skeptical of outsiders. Their settlements are self-sustaining, and they pride themselves on their ability to protect their own. Their thieves, assassins and spy networks are unparalleled since the Yamondulo.

TRADITIONS

POISONED OATHS

Vengeance pacts are commonly sworn by individuals for personal sleights and by Zadzisai secret networks for wrongdoing against their people.

THE MAKING

A coming-of-age tradition where youths must build something of lasting value.

INOCULATION

Following The Making, all youths are required to experience the effects of and then be inoculated against every poison in their tribal lexicon.